For Fred

HARRY'S BATH
A Bantam Little Rooster Book/August 1990

Little Rooster is a trademark of Bantam Books,
a division of Bantam Doubleday Dell Publishing Group, Inc.

Library of Congress Cataloging-in-Publication Data
Ziefert, Harriet.
Harry's bath/by Harriet Ziefert; illustrated by Seymour Chwast.
p. cm.
"A Bantam little rooster book."
Summary: Harry tries to explain to his mother how various animals in the bathtub
are preventing him from taking a bath himself.
ISBN 0-553-05863-0
[1. Baths—Fiction.] I. Chwast, Seymour, ill. II. Title.   [E]—dc20
89-17548
CIP
AC

Published simultaneously in the United States and Canada

Bantam Books are published by Bantam Books, a division of Bantam Doubleday Dell
Publishing Group, Inc. Its trademark, consisting of the words "Bantam Books" and the
portrayal of a rooster, is Registered in U.S. Patent and Trademark Office and in other
countries. Marca Registrada, Bantam Books, 666 Fifth Avenue, New York, NY 10103.

PRINTED IN SINGAPORE FOR HARRIET ZIEFERT, INC.

0 9 8 7 6 5 4 3 2 1

Harry's Bath

By Harriet Ziefert

Illustrated by Seymour Chwast

A BANTAM LITTLE ROOSTER BOOK

NEW YORK · TORONTO · LONDON · SYDNEY · AUCKLAND

Harry looked like he was ready for his bath.

"Harry, are you in the tub yet?"
called Harry's mother
from downstairs.

"Not yet, Mom," answered Harry. "There's a bear in my bath."

"Harry, you're being silly.
Get into the tub."

"Mom, I'm not being silly.
A dinosaur and a cow
are in my bath, too!"

"Harry, I'm coming upstairs
to see what you're doing."

"Mom, I'm in...

and out of the tub!"

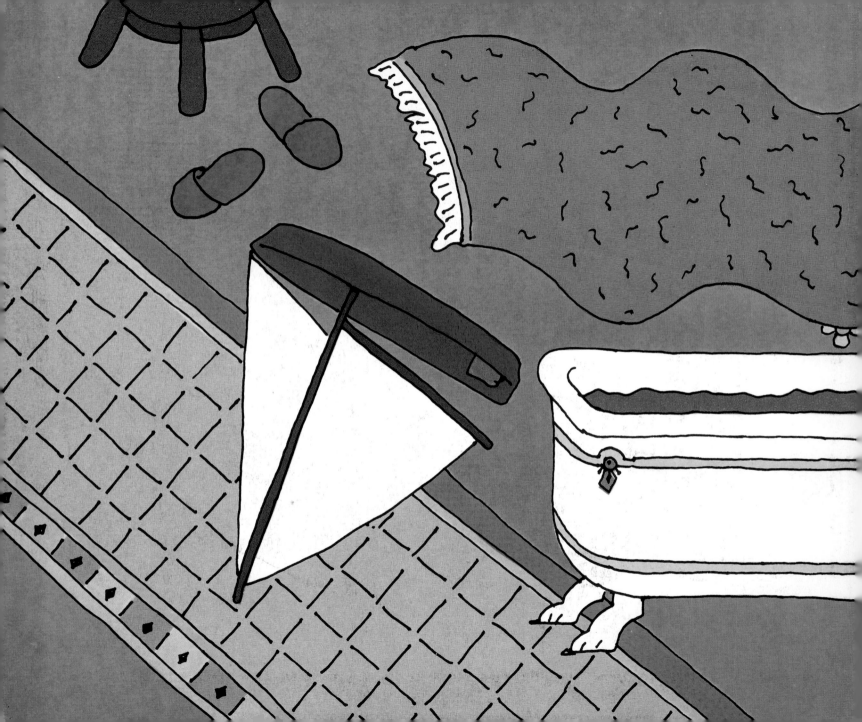